W9-CCW-558

BRONWEN, *the* TRAW, *and the* SHAPE-SHIFTER

A POEM IN FOUR PARTS BY

JAMES DICKEY

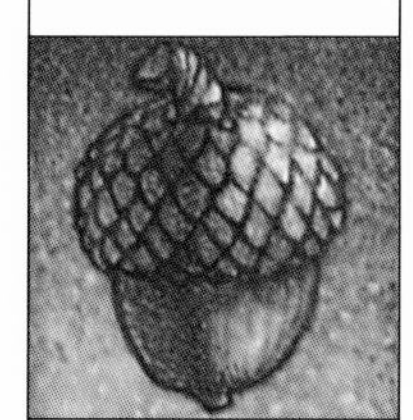
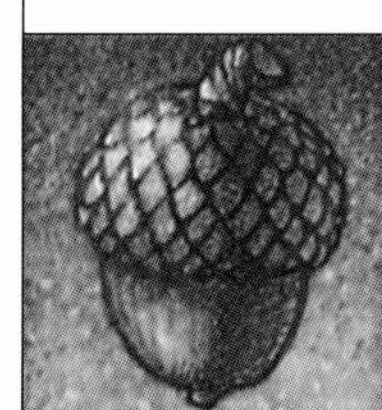

ILLUSTRATED BY

RICHARD JESSE WATSON

Bruccoli Clark

Harcourt Brace Jovanovich, Publishers

San Diego New York London

Library of Congress Cataloging-in-Publication Data
Dickey, James.
Bronwen, the traw, and the shape-shifter.
Summary: A narrative poem in which a young girl
battles with the elements she finds in the night.
1. Children's poetry, American. [1. Night—Poetry.
2. Narrative poetry. 3. American poetry] I. Watson,
Richard Jesse, ill. II. Title.
PS3554.I32B7 1986 811'.54 85-27082
ISBN 0-15-212580-9

The illustrations in this book were done on Strathmore illustration
board using a glazing of Winsor Newton transparent water colours,
with a pinch of Prisma pencil.
The text type was set via the Linotron 202 in Cochin Roman with Cloister Italic by
Thompson Type, San Diego, California.
The display type was photoset in Cochin by Thompson Type,
San Diego, California.
Color separations were made by Heinz Weber, Inc., Los Angeles, California.
Printed by Rae Publishing Company, Inc., Cedar Grove, New Jersey.
Bound by A. Horowitz & Sons, Bookbinders, Fairfield, New Jersey.
Production supervision by Warren Wallerstein.
Designed by Joy Chu.

Printed in the United States of America
First edition
A B C D E

HBJ

TO BRONWEN AND HER MOTHER
IN THE ELEMENTS

— J. D.

FOR JESU, JOY OF MY DESIRING

— R. J. W.

B O O K   O N E

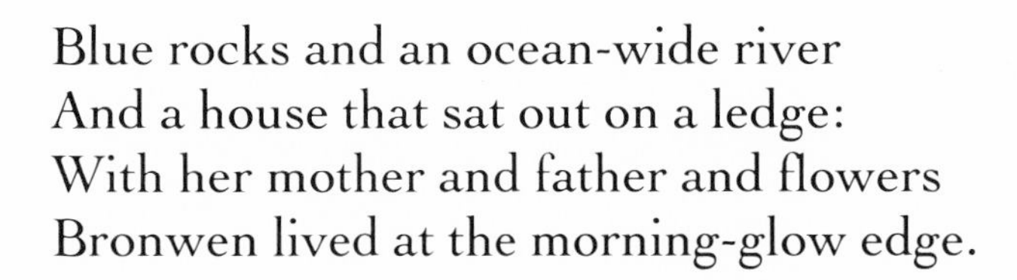

Blue rocks and an ocean-wide river
And a house that sat out on a ledge:
With her mother and father and flowers
Bronwen lived at the morning-glow edge.

From the window she'd look out at daybreak
Deep into the brimming blue haze
That, while her blue eyes stood watching,
Burned away in the river's far blaze.

Her mother'd look up from her planting
In her light-blowing dahlia blouse
As Bronwen came over the flagstones
In her sunflower hat from the house.

She would kneel in the brown of the garden
With the pines and their jack-strawing straw
And dig round the roses and tulips
With the tingling three prongs of her traw.

The traw was a kind of a trowel
But her dad made it curve like a claw,
And cut out with tin-snips the fingers
Of the world's only really real traw.

The fat worms knew she meant business,
As, with ointment of zinc on her nose,
She dug for the magical color
That comes up through the stem of the rose.

But when sun passed the bee-wingèd greenhouse
Growing big and red, less and less bright,
She would lift up her eyes from the rose bed
And look round, in the less and less light.

The grass would grow dark, and the flowers,
And the sun disappear in a field
Off yonder where roads came together
And the light in the river was sealed,

And the All-Dark would rise from the hedges
On its single dim monsterous foot,
And walk in thick steps from the orchard
And through the high bedrooms like soot.

Brownwen knew that the All-Dark would find her
As it did in its path every night;
It would come as though coming behind her
And blank everything else out of sight.

For the All-Dark was more than the evening,
And wasn't the worst thing of all,
For the All-Dark turned loose the Shape-Shifter,
And stood and looked in from the hall.

Where the cracks of her blue door went lightless
The All-Dark took charge of the wall;
It hung like the wrong side of brightness,
And was nothing, and more than the wall.

It lies like a great bed of nothing,
It stands on the floor and the chair,
It rides the strange square of the window,
And is everything there that is there.

It builds itself high like a cliffside,
It layers itself like a cake,
In children's dim rooms like a half-world
It stands all around till they wake.

But that's not the worst of the All-Dark,
Though its silence is part of the worst;
The worst is the Shapes that come from it,
And the last is as bad as the first.

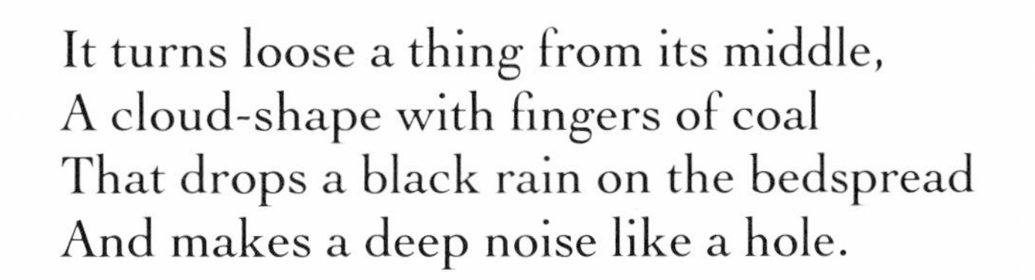

It turns loose a thing from its middle,
A cloud-shape with fingers of coal
That drops a black rain on the bedspread
And makes a deep noise like a hole.

In the fall when the window is rattling,
It's the shape a dark air-shape would have
If it turned itself topsy-turvy
And blew from a terrible cave.

From its side grows a red hand of fire
With its fingers more dreadful to see
Than the spiked slow leaves of the fly-trap
When they close round the wings of the bee.

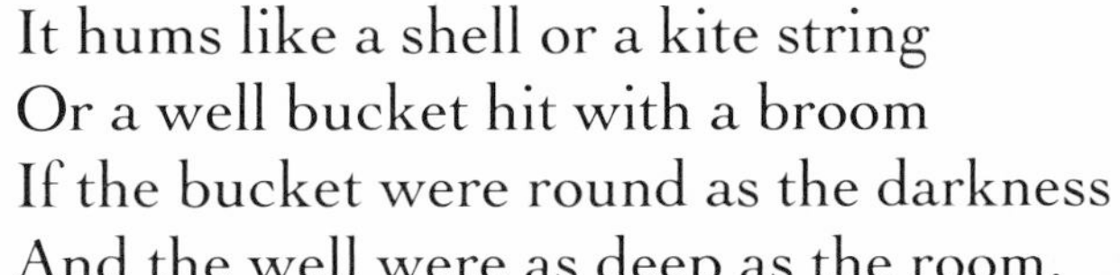

It hums like a shell or a kite string
Or a well bucket hit with a broom
If the bucket were round as the darkness
And the well were as deep as the room.

BOOK TWO

In the ring of the All-Dark lay Bronwen
With the pane on one side, and the moon
With the four Shape-Shifters emerging
And making their moves one by one.

But a light knock came on the window
A knock like the tail of a kite,
A sound not made by the All-Dark
Or by any wrong shape of the night.

No other knock came on the glass-dark
But Bronwen looked out toward the rap
That a leaf might have made in its falling
And the stem turned around with a tap.

A shadow stood up looking inward,
And was there, not trying to pass,
A shape like the shape of a mitten
That changed the whole life of the glass.

The fur of its shade ruffled softly
As it held the far side of the chill.
Who would let such a soft thing stay warmless?
Bronwen lifted the sash from the sill.

In glided a spread-open squirrel
With its eyes not taken from her.
It looked like the ones of her garden,
But it sat, and then folded its fur.

It came down to rest on her bed-foot
But she couldn't feel it at all,
For she couldn't imagine or make up
Anything so light, graceful and small.

At the window more squirrels were shadowed;
They sailed in, but with never one wing,
And the one on her bedspread said nothing,
But in a leaf's voice started to sing.

"Are you Bronwen of the Blue Cliffs,
Of the garden and the sun?
Are you Bronwen of your parents
And their one and only one?

"Are you Bronwen of the roses,
And the crow's split-level caw?
Are you Bronwen of the fountain?
Are you Bronwen of the traw?"

I am Bronwen Bronwen Bronwen,
I am Bronwen of the hose
I am Bronwen of the sprinkler
I am Bronwen of the rose.

I am Bronwen Bronwen Bronwen
I am Bronwen most of all,
I am Bronwen when I do and when I don't.
I am Bronwen of the blue eyes
I am Bronwen of the cliffs
I am Bronwen when I will and when I won't.

I am Bronwen Bronwen Bronwen,
I am Bronwen all the time
I am Bronwen with three freckles on my nose
I am Bronwen of the rabbit
I am Bronwen of the wren
I am Bronwen from my pigtails to my toes.

I am Bronwen Bronwen Bronwen
I am Bronwen once again.
When you see me you are glad at what you saw.
I am Bronwen of the fountain
Of the river rose once more
I am Bronwen of the blue eyes and the traw.

"You must come with us in moonlight,
You must glide with us and cross
The wide grey star-bright river
In a shawl of riding moss."

But you are only squirrels
No matter how you try;
You are only mitten-squirrels,
And you can't even fly!

"We can't fly like hawks and eagles,
We can't go where condors go,
But on silver nights of autumn
We glide down and down like snow.

"We are flying squirrels only
But we float like thistledown.
We ride like every wind there is
Where every wind has flown.

"We must take you to our country,
We must lift you like a ghost.
You must take a magic weapon,
The thing you love the most.

"It can't be big and scary,
It must have its own right name:
The most loved and the most you use,
For these are both the same.

"You must wear a hat that makes you
The Bronwen of the sun,
And that turns you around like a flower
To light the All-Darkening One."

I'll go if you will take me
Bronwen said, *and I will cross*
With my traw the wide grey river
In a shawl of moon and moss.

In a net of threads they set her,
In a room gone more than still;
In light tree-wool they lifted
And launched out from the sill.

The river grew in greyness
As the cliff fell from them where
They rode on simple air alone
That was there and there and there.

Through the moss she watched the stars stay,
Amazing where they stood;
In moss she traveled free and clear
Through a wild and rootless wood.

For gliding is not walking
And is better than them all;
When you ride with flying squirrels
You cannot ever fall.

So Bronwen lay back watching
The stars move through the threads;
All children should have such delight
When they look out from their beds.

They should see the gentle ruffling fur
Of squirrels at their ease
Upholding them in gentle air
In the swaying strings of trees.

They sank to the far Earth so gently
That there was no change in the air;
They touched the low leap of a hilltop
And came to rest cradling, just there.

It was the softest green country
That a moss-bed in flight ever felt;
If there'd've been more softness, even,
It would have had reason to melt.

The squirrel who'd sat on her bed-foot
In her home on the high steady stone
Brought a kingly great squirrel to meet her
And she took his gold paw in her own.

"We have brought you far over the water
Because we are living in fear.
You may think this the gentlest of countries
But a one-footed terror lives here.

"Its name is the great-spreading All-Dark
And it falls on us here in the East
Where the sun rolls away to the westward
And leaves us to each secret beast.

"The weasels can find us, and night hawks,
From the snakes we go rigid with fright,
And we fall to the owls and the wildcats
And all things that can see without light.

"We have heard that you have in your garden
A tool like a marvelous claw
That can take on our own kind of magic."
Bronwen said, *It's all true. It's my traw.*

But how did you hear that I had it?
And I SURELY don't know how to fight!
"The hat on your blond head turns sunward
And against all the force of the night."

But how did you know I was living
Where the rock rises up from the rock?
And how did you know just which window,
And just how to knock, and not knock?

"The sea gull told us, the robin,
And the wren and the red butterfly;
All the wings that come over the river
And do their best things in the sky."

I'll do what you asked me to come for
Bronwen said, *but where must I go?*
"First to the bright turning fountain
Where the waters rise up as they flow.

"Then you'll fight in the Rocky Arena,
The All-Dark's main cave and his lair.
It's like a great hole and a quarry,
And the Shape-Shifter lives with him there."

In a clearing the fountain was turning
And the squirrels placed Bronwen inside.
She stood still as the live drops went round her
Like a ring she could center with pride.

She gazed through the high rounding water
And the shapes that danced there like the moon
Were angels and horses and dolphins
That went and came back as they spun.

And sometimes they danced all together
So the horse and the dolphin were one
And you could not tell running from swimming
Or how this bright mystery was done.

She held up the traw to the sparkle,
To the bend of the high looping lines,
And three drops fell misting together
On the traw, and its three tingling tines.

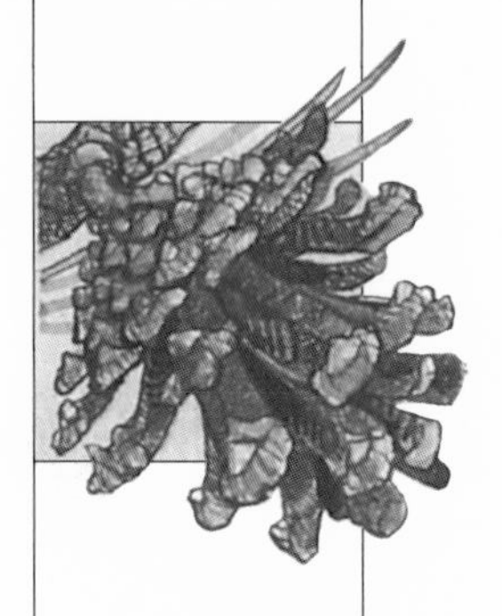

A sea gull sent one, and a llama;
The tines of the traw took their glow;
From the horse and the dolphin, the other
As they leapt in the flash and the flow.

The shape of the angel so flickered
That you couldn't be sure it was there:
It was quick, it was gone, it was coming,
The thinnest light-shape in the air,

But a spark would flash out like a feather
Or like something some deep hand had stirred,
Its movement so quick and so fleeting
It could come from no earth-wingèd bird.

And the squirrels then lifted out Bronnie
From the fountain that turned like a wheel
With the three touched tines of her weapon
That now had a quickened new feel.

"Are you game for the rocks and the darkness?"
The King of the Squirrels said then.
Yes I am, and for the Shape-Shifter,
Bronwen said, *just show where and say when.*

"Where the blackness is blacker than any,
Like a great open mouth, like a jaw,
You must do what you can with your gumption
And your sunflower hat and your traw."

She was there, in the stone-blinded silence,
And listened, and heard nothing stir;
But a sound like a low-brimming whisper
Rose then, and came toward her.

In a second she was high in a whirlwind,
She was upside down, turning like straw,
But her hat stayed in place, although cockeyed,
And she held to her fountainous traw.

Touch the root, touch the root, she kept saying:
If I can just tumble and find
Where the foot whirls alone on the wild ground
I can cut all the strength from the wind.

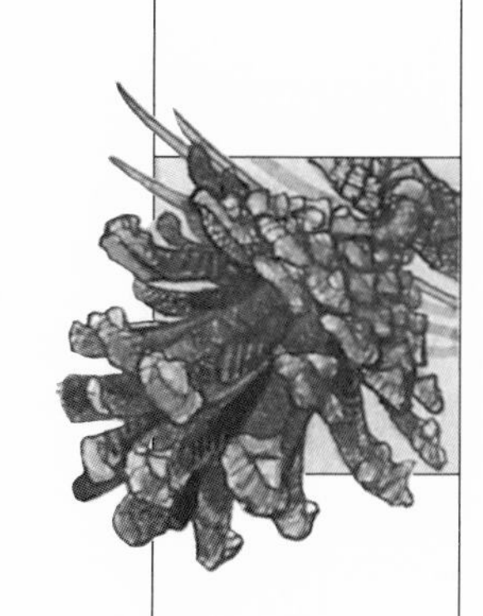

And she swanned herself out like a diver
Spinning down through that buffeting hall
And touched the crazed foot of the air-beast
And the wind fell off, and let fall.

Bronwen picked herself up from the gravel,
From the sharp stony soil of that bed;
She had got only strawberried elbows
But one tine of the traw had gone dead.

All the stone now glowed like a foundry
Like the claw-hammered steel of a forge;
Smoke poured from the jaws of the rock-face
And filled all the grim of the gorge.

Fire leapt out for Bronwen and found her;
She gasped, and she started to choke
As the animal-flame went around her
And tears came to her from the smoke.

Touch the blue, touch the blue, she said gamely,
For I broke the wind's strength at the root,
And she leaned and struck down with her prong-tool
The torch-purple fan of the foot.

The fire lost its circle and passion
And the smoke lost its black lungs for good;
There were only ashes and embers
In the ring where smudged Bronnie stood.

I have only one tine from the fountain,
Bronwen thought, and looked down; it was true —
The water had blessed the three fingers;
She had one, but she still needed two.

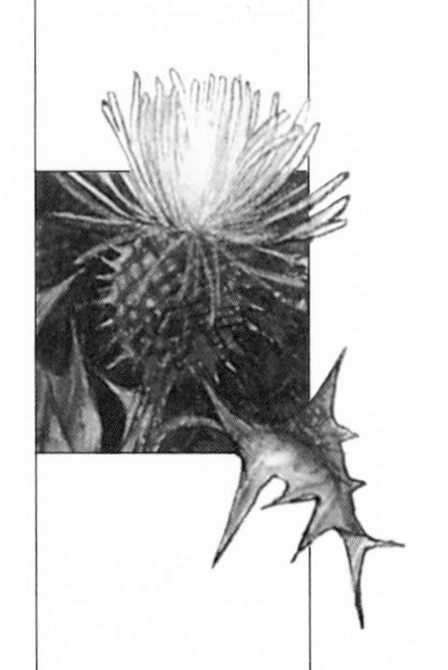

The All-Dark gives no time for waiting;
When it fails it comes right back again.
A great tidal wave sprang for Bronnie
That the rocks had held somewhere within.

Her feet were swept out from under
And she hung in the curve of a wave;
The bottom-sand swirled up around her
Like the grains in a dust-devil's cave.

The foot of this thing moves too swiftly,
Bronwen thought, as she struggled for breath,
I can't do what I did with the others
For this foot is more deadly than death.

I must somehow get up to the topside
To save what I'm trying to save;
I must reap the wild white of the water,
For a wave with no crest is no wave.

With her dog-paddle strokes and her hat down
On her ears like an umbrella-flower,
Bronwen frog-leggèd up the green smash-wall
And reached the white line of its power.

Along this she sped like a sunfish;
Like the triple-toothed blade of a saw
As the crest of the wave was reaped helpless
Was the last rushing tine of her traw.

The wave sank down into sand-dust;
Like a shell, dripping Bronwen rolled there
With her traw bent, flattened, and corkscrewed
And the water gone safe as the air.

BOOK FOUR

But beneath her two feet there then opened
The endless deep black of the earth;
Though Bronwen stood fast, she knew surely
That this was death's go-for-broke birth.

"Come back, leap back, gutsy Bronwen,
For your traw has gone dead in your hand;
You cannot fight the mad suck-hole
That can take the whole life of the land."

No, I'll stand once again, said blond Bronwen,
I'll stand with my traw and my hat;
I'll stand, for the world's frightened children;
If it's that, it'll have to be that.

Bronwen felt herself going under
As beneath a black bodiless tongue;
She was swallowed without any warning
And down useless darkness was flung.

Her traw almost left her forever
As she sank in this most deadly calm;
But the handle she'd taken for granted
Was a new living blaze in her palm,

For something had touched it in passing
When the horses and dolphins had dashed
And the fountain had spun like a river
And the light drops had misted and flashed.

A heat came into her fingers
As, from the dazzled dead tines,
The handle turned round and was with her
Like a lightning-struck crest of dry pines.

What had touched it was father or feather,
Or what had just thought it was there;
It was angel or bird mixed with water,
Or a one-lifetime trick of the air,

But the flash from the quick of the fountain
Found the mud at the glut of its suck
And the earth healed entirely around her
And some was just guts, and some luck,

For she rose in the lightening stone-space
Now like a rock garden she knew,
And Bronwen had beaten the dark back
With her eyes of bluebonnet blue.

The King of the Squirrels came to her
Where she stood with her beaten-up traw
And took her light hand laced with scratches
In the royal gold gold of his paw.

"You have beaten the All-Dark forever:
All his height and his breadth and his length,
For, huge as he is, he is nothing:
The Shifter was all of his strength.

"The snake and the weasel drew from him,
From his earth, water, fire, and air;
Against these our efforts were futile;
We could never find someone who'd dare

"To face the Four Forms in the open;
We were many, but weaker than few;
Now the All-Dark will keep the Shapes hidden
And will sleep as the rest of us do."

You're welcome, said Bronwen, and curtsied,
What a hard-working night THIS has been!
I can't say "There was nothing to it,"
And I sure wouldn't do it again!

"To get you back over the river
We'll have to use muscle and wit
For you live on a cliff-top already
And we'll need to get higher than it.

"We have a steep mountain, and from it
A single pine tree rises high;
It's the best that we've got, and the nearest
This country can get to the sky.

"So you and my best-gliding squirrels
Must climb to the top branches there
So we can create our own angle
And invent the right downslope of air."

At home, Bronwen said, *there's a cupboard,*
Very tall, where they keep my pink cup.
I learned to climb anything that way,
Anything in the world that goes up.

I love to go higher and higher;
Dad says that when I make my moves
I can get up on anything standing:
Bookcases, broom-closets and stoves.

So don't fret about me and your hilltop
And the climb to the top of your tree,
For a trunk and some limbs on a mountain
Will be less than a chair-back to me.

So she and the King's twenty squirrels
Climbed and clung where the top branches shook
And the green peace was boundless, and living,
And was everywhere Bronwen could look.

A fresh net of moss came together;
Bronwen lay in its fragrant new weave
And the Squirrels, grasping all its light edges,
Spread the fur of their light sides, to leave.

Let me have one more look, cried Bronwen,
Though her eyelids were wearing her out;
The whole land took over her memory,
And they were the same, just about.

From the twigs that were smallest and highest
Where Bron in the whole country slept
The squirrels took aim upon distance
And lifted their sleeper, and leapt.

They slid from the top of the country
Where Bronwen had won what she'd won,
Her sunflower hat pulled down over
Her eyes, to keep out the sun.

One or two grey glimpses of river
Where sunrise burned vivid and pale
Were all that Bronwen remembered
Of her journey home, and one sail

Like a butterfly-pinch on the water
Where she dreamt in her squirrel-borne loom
And the blue cliffs rose high and brought to her
The flowered blue walls of her room.

Her mother and father'd not missed her,
For she was the same as she'd been
As she came down the stairs to the flagstones
And was part of the same morning scene.

But the earth of the garden was kinder;
Underfoot it could never give way;
It held up the tulips and dahlias
Just enough, and the roses would stay

Where they wished to, in no earthly danger
Because Bron had been where she'd been,
And the sheaf of the rainbowing sprinkler
Turned round like a fountain she'd seen.

The breeze stirred the stems and the flowers,
The best that could happen to air;
You'd not think that a one-footed demon,
Turned loose, had ever spun there.

On the hearth the embers glowed deeply;
Bronwen gazed with their warmth on her face,
Or sometimes read, or played checkers
With every red disc in its place.

She liked the red checkers better;
She built kings at the enemy's back,
And she and the flames played together
Against the always-beat black.

And then, when the last embers shifted,
And All-Quiet came to the walls
Bronwen climbed up the stairs to her bedroom
And turned out the lights in the halls.

With all children safe from the Shifter
And the traw's dented glow on the shelf
Bronwen slept like lilies and dahlias
And the All-Dark slept in itself.

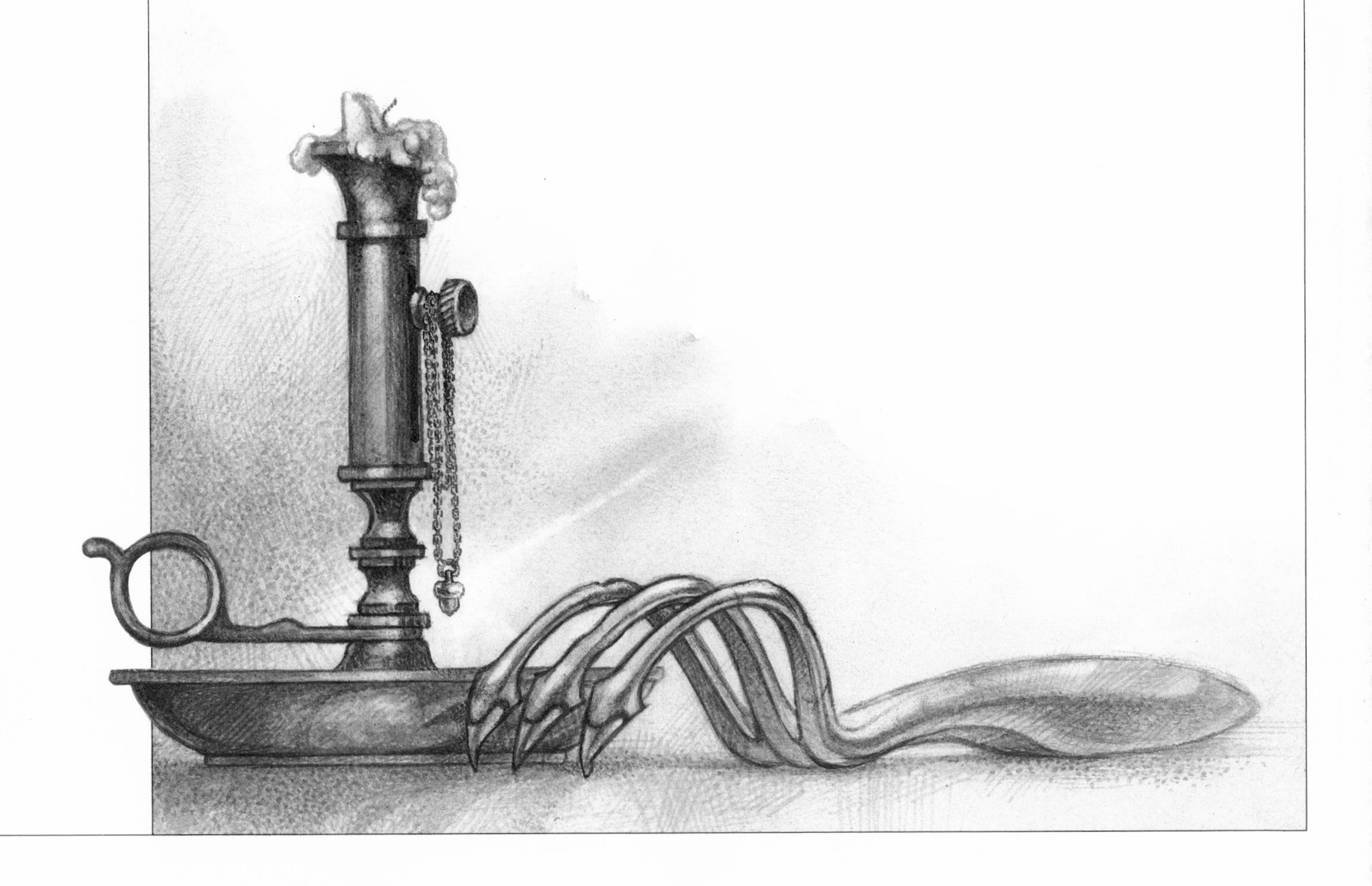